The Winning Pony

Do you love ponies? Be a Pony Pal!

Look for these Pony Pal books:

#1 I Want a Pony
#2 A Pony for Keeps
#3 A Pony in Trouble
#4 Give Me Back My Pony
#5 Pony to the Rescue
#6 Too Many Ponies
#7 Runaway Pony
#8 Good-bye Pony
#9 The Wild Pony
Super Special #1 The Baby Pony
#10 Don't Hurt My Pony
#11 Circus Pony
#12 Keep Out, Pony!
#13 The Girl Who Hated Ponies
#14 Pony-Sitters
Super Special #2 The Story of Our Ponies
#15 The Blind Pony
#16 The Missing Pony Pal
#17 Detective Pony
#18 The Saddest Pony
#19 Moving Pony
#20 Stolen Ponies

coming soon

#22 Western Pony

The Winning Pony

Jeanne Betancourt

illustrated by Vivien Kubbos

SCHOLASTIC INC.
New York Toronto London Auckland Sydney
Mexico City New Delhi Hong Kong

ISBN 0-590-63405-4

Published by Scholastic Inc., 555 Broadway, New York, NY 10012, by arrangement with Scholastic Australia Pty Limited.

12 11 10 9 8 7 6 5 4 3 2 9/9 0 1 2 3 4/0

Printed in the U.S.A. **40**

First Scholastic printing, July 1999

Cover and text illustrations by Vivien Kubbos
Typeset in Bookman

Contents

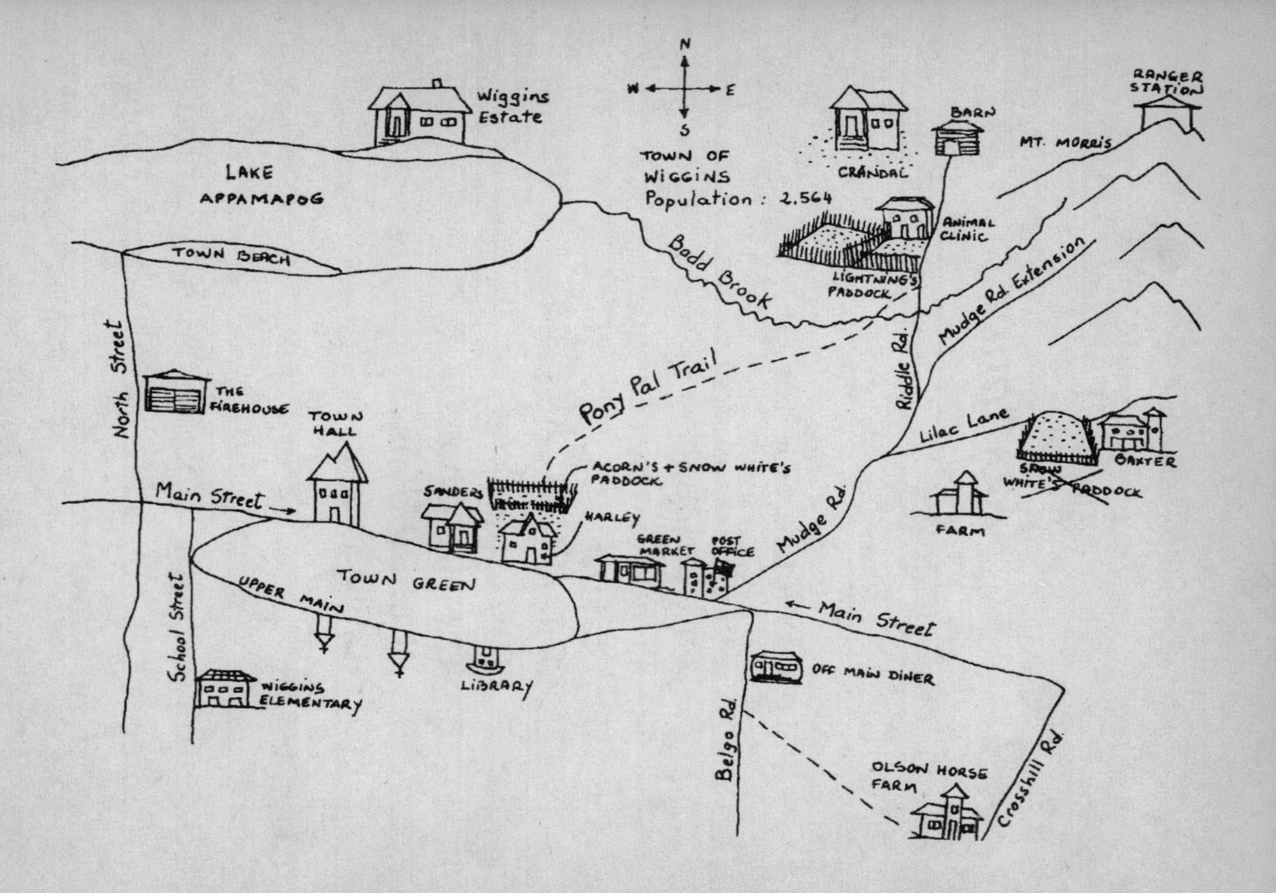

N
W
E
S
TOWN OF WIGGINS
Population : 2,564
Wiggins Estate
LAKE APPAMAPOG
TOWN BEACH
CRANDAL
BARN
RANGER STATION
MT. MORRIS
ANIMAL CLINIC
LIGHTNING'S PADDOCK
Badd Brook
Mudge Rd. Extension
Riddle Rd.
Pony Pal Trail
North Street
THE FIREHOUSE
TOWN HALL
Main Street
SANDERS
ACORN'S + SNOW WHITE'S PADDOCK
HARLEY
Lilac Lane
SNOW WHITE'S PADDOCK
BAXTER
FARM
Mudge Rd.
GREEN MARKET
POST OFFICE
TOWN GREEN
UPPER MAIN
School Street
WIGGINS ELEMENTARY
LIBRARY
Main Street
OFF MAIN DINER
Belgo Rd.
OLSON HORSE FARM
Crosshill Rd.

Save the Shelter

Pam Crandal led her pony to the barn. "Time to saddle up," she told Lightning. "We're going to meet our Pony Pals." Lightning nickered happily as if to say, "Great."

Pam was brushing Lightning when her mother came into the barn. Mrs. Crandal stroked the upside-down heart on Lightning's forehead. "Morning, pretty pony," she said. Lightning gently nuzzled Mrs. Crandal's shoulder. "Pam, you have a wonderful pony here," her mother said.

Pam laid her head on Lightning's side. "I know," she said.

"Where are you two going today?" Mrs. Crandal asked.

"I'm meeting Anna and Lulu at the diner," Pam answered. "Then we're going for a trail ride."

"Could you girls ride over to St. Francis Animal Shelter for me?" Mrs. Crandal asked. "I have some horse show posters for them."

"Sure," Pam told her mother. "I love going there." She smoothed Lightning's saddle blanket over the pony's back. "I think it's great that you're putting on a horse show to raise money for homeless animals."

"Are you going to be in the horse show?" her mother asked.

"Anna and Lulu want to," Pam answered. "But not me. I don't like horse shows that much."

"When I was your age my friend Eleanor and I loved horse shows," Mrs. Crandal said. "We still do."

"I'd rather just ride for fun," Pam told her mother. "Not for prizes."

"But horse shows are fun," Mrs. Crandal said. "And there's nothing wrong with prizes. Look at Eleanor. She became an Olympic jumping star."

"Yeah, I know," Pam said as she tightened Lightning's girth.

Pam liked her mother's friend, Eleanor Morgan. Eleanor traveled all over the world with her horse, Starfire. Starfire was a chestnut Thoroughbred with a white star marking on his forehead. Pam thought Starfire was the most magnificent horse she had ever seen.

"Eleanor e-mailed me this morning," Mrs. Crandal told Pam. "She's finished her European tour. She might come and visit us."

"Will she bring Starfire?" Pam asked.

"I don't know," her mother answered.

While Pam led Lightning out of the barn Mrs. Crandal went for the posters. Pam put them in her saddle bags, mounted and rode off.

Half an hour later she walked into Off-Main Diner. Anna and Lulu were already sitting in the Pony Pals' favorite booth. Anna's mother owned the diner, so the three girls went there a lot.

Pam went over to the booth and the girls decided what they wanted for breakfast. Pam and Lulu went to the counter for glasses of milk and Anna put in their order for blueberry pancakes. While they ate, Anna and Lulu talked about the horse show. "It's going to be so much fun," Anna told Pam.

"I can't wait," said Lulu. "Snow White loves horse shows."

"So does Acorn," added Anna. "What events should we enter?"

Anna and Lulu decided that they would compete in Equitation Walk, Trot and Canter.

"Let's do jumping, too," said Lulu. "Then we have a chance at the championship trophy. That would be so cool."

"What about you, Pam?" Lulu asked.

"I'm not competing," Pam told them.

"But you and Lightning are such great jumpers," protested Anna.

"I bet you could win the championship," added Lulu.

"I love jumping, but not in a horse show," Pam explained.

"But this horse show is for such a good cause," Lulu said.

"St. Francis Animal Shelter needs money to take care of all the animals they rescue," added Anna.

"I'll help with the show," Pam said. "But I'm not competing."

"I wish you'd be in it, too," said Anna. "Maybe you'll change your mind."

"I don't think so," Pam said.

Pam saw Mimi Kline, Rosalie Lacey and Mrs. Kline coming towards the diner. She pointed out the window. "Look who's here," she said.

Mimi saw the Pony Pals and waved. Mimi was five years old and her friend Rosalie was six. They were both horse crazy. Rosalie wanted a pony more than anything in the world. Mimi had her own pony, Tongo.

Mrs. Kline and the two girls came into the diner. "I'm going to be in the horse show," Mimi shouted as she ran towards the Pony Pals. "Tongo and me." She squeezed into the booth next to Anna. "Mommy said I could."

Rosalie sat next to Pam. Pam noticed that she looked upset. She leant towards the younger girl. "What's wrong, Rosalie?" she asked.

"I can't be in the horse show," Rosalie whispered in Pam's ear. "I don't have a pony."

Pam felt sorry for Rosalie. Her mother wouldn't let her have any pets. Mrs. Lacey said they couldn't afford them. But Pam thought the real reason was that Mrs. Lacey didn't like animals.

Mrs. Kline pulled up a chair and sat down at the end of the booth. "We saw your ponies outside and stopped by to see you," she

said. "I was wondering if you thought Tongo and Mimi could be in the horse show."

"They could be in Lead Line," Pam told her. "But Mimi should practice for it."

"Could you girls work with her?" Mrs. Kline asked. "You helped her so much when we first bought Tongo."

Pam and Anna exchanged a smile. The small pony and his owner were both a handful. But working with them had still been fun.

"Okay," Anna told Mrs. Kline. "We'll help."

"We're going to get a blue ribbon," Mimi said excitedly. "Me and Tongo."

"Maybe Rosalie can ride Tongo in the horse show, too," Pam suggested.

"Rosalie is older and more experienced," added Lulu. "She could enter the Walk, Trot class."

"Certainly Rosalie can ride Tongo," agreed Mrs. Kline. "We'll just have to be sure it's okay with her mother. I'll speak to her about it."

Mimi clapped her hands. "Yea," she shouted. "We can both win ribbons."

Rosalie looked up at Pam with a grateful smile. "Can we have a lesson today?" she asked excitedly.

Pam looked over at Anna and Lulu. They both nodded.

"Sure," said Pam. "But first we have to deliver something to St. Francis Animal Shelter."

Lulu explained to Mimi and Rosalie that an animal shelter was a place for animals that didn't have a home.

"They mostly have cats and dogs," Pam said. "But sometimes they have other animals like rabbits and goats. They try to find new homes for the animals."

Anna told them that the money from the horse show would go to the shelter.

"I think I'll take the girls over there now," Mrs. Kline said. "Then they can see an animal shelter for themselves."

"We'll meet you there," Pam told her.

"Goodie!" exclaimed Mimi.

"I love animals," Rosalie told Pam. "All kinds of animals."

Mrs. Kline bought the girls ice-cream cones while the Pony Pals cleared the table.

"I'm going to be number one!" Pam heard Mimi telling her mother. "Tongo and me are going to win a blue ribbon."

That's why I don't like horse shows, thought Pam. Everybody wants to be number one. But only one person can win that blue ribbon. What will happen if Mimi isn't number one?

Chicago

The Pony Pals left the diner. They were unhitching their ponies when Mrs. Kline and the two girls came out. The younger girls came over to say hi to the ponies. Acorn eyed the ice-cream cones and took a step towards them.

"Watch your ice-cream cones!" Anna warned.

Mimi and Rosalie backed away and giggled.

Mrs. Kline came up to Pam and whispered in her ear. "Thank you for including Rosalie in the lessons with Tongo. She just came back from visiting her father in Chicago. She had a good time, but now she misses him more than ever. The divorce has been hard on her."

"Come on, come on," Mimi called to her mother. "We have to see the animals at the animal hotel."

Mrs. Kline explained that it was called an animal shelter, not an animal hotel, and led them to the car. The Pony Pals mounted their ponies and headed down Belgo Road. A few minutes later they turned their ponies onto a short-cut trail.

As they rode through the woods Pam thought how lucky she was that her parents loved animals as much as she did. Her mother was a riding teacher and her father was a veterinarian. The Crandals had lots of pets and Pam had a pony of her own for as long as she could remember.

Anna Harley didn't have her own pony until she was ten years old. But she had been riding at the Crandals' since she and

Pam met in kindergarten. Anna didn't like school as much as Pam. She was dyslexic, so reading and writing were difficult subjects for her. Anna was a terrific artist. She liked to look at art and draw, as much as Pam liked to read and write.

Pam and Anna had only known Lulu Sanders since the beginning of fifth grade. Lulu's mother died when Lulu was four. After that Lulu traveled all over the world with her dad. He was a naturalist, who wrote about wild animals. But when Lulu turned ten, her father said she should live in one place for a while. That's when Lulu moved to Wiggins. She lived with her grandmother in a house next to Anna's house. Now Lulu had a pony, too, and Acorn and Snow White shared a paddock behind the Harleys'.

Lulu knew more about animals than Pam and Anna. She had studied all kinds of animals with her father. Lulu loved to visit St. Francis Animal Shelter.

The Klines' car was already parked at

the shelter when the Pony Pals arrived. The three girls hitched their ponies to the fence and went inside the main building.

When they came through the door of the shelter, Mimi ran up to them. "They have dogs and cats and three goats and not enough room," she said in an excited whisper. "And somebody threw away kittens, but they're saved."

Rosalie and Mrs. Kline were looking into a cage at the back of the office. Mrs. Kline motioned for the Pony Pals. "Come see these adorable kittens," she said.

Rosalie was staring into the box. "Poor little kitties," she whispered. "Little, little kitties."

Pam looked over Rosalie's shoulder and saw three tiny, black-and-white kittens.

"They look too young to be separated from their mother," Lulu said.

"They miss their mommy," explained Mimi.

Rosalie looked up at Pam. She had tears in her eyes. "They miss their daddy, too," she said. "They need a place to live. They need someone to take care of them."

Mimi pointed to the smallest kitten. "That's the one Rosalie wants," she said.

"It's a boy cat," Rosalie told the Pony Pals. "The shelter lady said so."

Mrs. Kline put an arm around Rosalie's shoulder. "You can't have a kitten, Rosalie," she said softly. "Your mother said no pets."

Rosalie put her finger through the cage, near the kitten's face. He reached up and licked it. "He needs me," Rosalie said.

"I'm sure the shelter will find that kitten a good home," Anna told Rosalie. "They're such sweet kitties."

"I'm his mommy, now," Rosalie said. "I have to take care of him."

Mrs. Kline and Pam exchanged a glance.

"Let's give your kitty a name," suggested Mimi.

"A special name," said Rosalie.

Mrs. Kline stood up. "It's time to go, girls," she said.

Rosalie shook her head, no.

"Time to go, girls," Mrs. Kline repeated.

Pam knew how stubborn Rosalie could be when she set her mind to something. And it would be difficult to get her mind off that kitten.

"It's time for your riding lesson, girls," Pam said.

Mimi jumped up. "Yes!" she said. "I want to ride Tongo."

Rosalie continued to play with the kitten.

Just then Ms. Raskins came through the back door. Lulu gave her the posters.

"Thank you," Ms. Raskins said. "We're so happy that you are raising money for us. We need another room for kennels. There are so many mistreated and abandoned pets." She patted Rosalie on the head. "This little girl wants to help by adopting a kitten."

Pam caught Ms. Raskins' attention and shook her head, no.

"But, of course, she has to check with her mother first," Ms. Raskins added.

"My mother will let me have him. I'll tell her. He's so-oo little. I have to take care of him." She petted the top of the kitten's head. "My daddy likes kitties."

"Let's go, Rosalie," Anna said.

"Tongo's waiting," added Lulu.

"And I have to get back to work," said Ms. Raskins.

"I know my kitty's name," Rosalie said. "His name is Chicago. My little Chicago."

"That's a funny name," Mimi said. "I like it."

Rosalie finally stood up. But as they left the shelter she turned around three times to wave goodbye to Chicago.

Pam felt sorrier than ever for Rosalie Lacey. She wondered if a riding lesson would take her mind off the little black-and-white kitten.

Bad Behavior

The Pony Pals rode their ponies back to town. When they reached the Town Green, Anna halted Acorn. Pam and Lulu pulled up beside them.

"Let's leave our ponies in the paddock at my house," suggested Anna. "There's more room there than at the Klines'."

"But let's take Lightning with us," said Pam. "While Mimi is having her lesson on Tongo, Rosalie can practice on Lightning."

"Good idea," agreed Anna. "That way she won't have to wait for her turn to ride Tongo."

“A riding lesson might take Rosalie’s mind off that kitten,” added Lulu.

Mimi and Rosalie were waiting for the Pony Pals in the Klines’ backyard.

Rosalie ran over to them. “Mimi is having the first lesson because it’s her pony,” she said unhappily. “Her mother lets her have pets.”

Pam noticed that Rosalie still looked sad. “You could practice on Lightning,” she told her. “Then, when Mimi finishes her lesson, you can ride Tongo.”

Rosalie put her arms around Lightning’s neck. “I’m going to ride you, Lightning,” she told the pony.

Suddenly, Tongo was running across the yard towards them. When he reached Rosalie he nudged her with his nose and whinnied as if to say, “Pay attention to me.” Everyone broke out laughing at the jealous little pony.

Anna led Tongo to the shelter. “We’re going to have a riding lesson,” she told him.

On the other side of the yard, Pam began

the riding lesson with Rosalie and Lightning. Rosalie had never ridden Lightning. Pam was surprised at how well the little girl rode. Rosalie sat tall and centered in the saddle, kept her heels down, and looked straight ahead. Her touch on the reins was soft but firm.

Anna and Lulu, however, were having a difficult time with Tongo and Mimi. Tongo wanted either to stop and eat grass or race ahead. Mimi loved it when Tongo raced ahead. She didn't seem to care whether she could control him or not.

"Do you want to be in the horse show?" Pam heard Lulu ask Mimi.

"Yes, yes," insisted Mimi. "I have to win the ribbon."

"Then you have to calm down," Lulu scolded. "Or Tongo will never behave."

Pam looked over at the little Shetland pony. He was pulling on the lead to eat the leaves of a bush. Tongo was stubborn, spoilt and adorable—just like his owner.

When Mimi finished her lesson, it was Rosalie's turn to ride Tongo.

Pam tried to teach Rosalie to be firm with Tongo. "It's important to know how to ride different ponies," Pam explained. Rosalie did her best, but she couldn't control the stubborn pony the way she could Lightning.

When the lessons were over, the Pony Pals went back to Anna's. They put Lightning in the paddock while they had lunch. The rest of the afternoon they rode the trails on Ms. Wiggins' estate. Ms. Wiggins was a friend of the Pony Pals, who kept miles of well-groomed trails. She told the Pony Pals that they could ride on her land whenever they wanted. They went there often.

After a long trail ride the three girls went back to Pam's for a picnic supper and a barn sleepover. They had their picnic on a big, flat rock next to the paddock. Woolie, the Crandals' dog, sat near Pam, waiting for scraps. Fat Cat and two of her kittens scampered around the field looking for mice.

"I hope we can make a lot of money for

the animal shelter," Lulu said. "They do such good work for needy animals."

"I wish we could get hundreds of people to come," said Anna. "That would raise a lot of money."

"It would help if we had some special event," Lulu said. "You know, like a rodeo performance or a special riding demonstration."

"Hey . . . I have an idea," exclaimed Pam. "We should ask Eleanor Morgan to help us."

"Who's she?" asked Lulu.

"Eleanor is a friend of Mrs. Crandal," explained Anna. "And an Olympic jumping champion. Pam has videotapes of her jumping. I even met her once. She's really nice."

"And she just came home from a big European tour," said Pam. "She lives about an hour's drive from here. My mother said she might visit us."

Lulu jumped up. "Let's see if your mother will ask her to be in the horse show," she said.

The three girls picked up their picnic things and ran to the barn. Mrs. Crandal was at her desk in the barn office. Pam told her their idea.

"That's a terrific idea," she said.

"Do you think she'll do it, Mrs. Crandal?" Anna asked.

"She might," answered Mrs. Crandal. "Eleanor has a heart of gold and she loves animals."

"Will you ask her?" Lulu said.

Mrs. Crandal thought for a second. "I think it would be better if you girls asked her," she answered. "You can e-mail her from my computer." She stood up. "I have to feed the school horses and ponies. You can do it right now."

Pam sat at her mother's desk and turned on the computer. "Let's all write to Eleanor," she said. "We can each use a different font. It'll look neat. She'll like that."

"Okay," agreed Lulu.

The Pony Pals took turns sitting at the

computer to write to Eleanor. They edited the message until they thought it was perfect.

Anna and Lulu looked over Pam's shoulder as they checked it one last time before sending it.

Dear Eleanor Morgan,

Hi. It's Pam Crandal. My Pony Pals and I are writing you about St. Francis Animal Shelter. They take care of cats, dogs and sometimes other animals that need a home. They try hard to find new homes for the animals. But there are still a lot of animals that live in the shelter. The shelter needs money. Mom and Mr. Olson are having a horse show at Mr. Olson's farm to raise money for the shelter. We wondered if you would do a jumping exhibition for the horse show. If you did, a lot of people would buy tickets to come and see you. All the money would go to the shelter.

Hi. I'm Pam's Pony Pal, Lulu Sanders. I

have a Welsh pony. Her name is Snow White. The show is on August 10th at 9 am. Mrs. Crandal hopes you will come. She told us all about the fun you had when you were our age. I bet you would have fun if you came to do the show.

Hi. My name is Anna Harley. I'm a Pony Pal, too. I met you once at Pam's. But it was a long time ago, so you probably don't remember me. I have my own pony now. His name is Acorn. I hope you get to meet him some day. We're going to be in a horse show next week.

Pam's mother said you and she were Pony Pals when you were our age. Is that true? If you were Pony Pals, I bet you would love to see each other again. Pony Pals stay friends forever. Please come.

St. Francis Animal Shelter needs you. It would make everyone happy if you said yes.

Sincerely, Pam, Lulu, Anna

That night Pam lay awake after her friends had fallen asleep. She remembered seeing Eleanor on television during the Olympics. Eleanor came third in jumping and won the bronze medal for America. Eleanor was a big star. Would she want to ride in their little horse show?

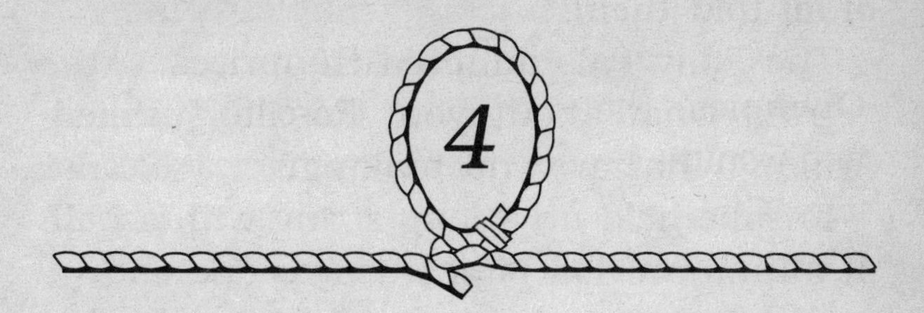

Troublesome Tongo

The first thing Pam did when she woke up the next morning was check for an e-mail message from Eleanor. There wasn't one.

After breakfast the girls rode back to Anna's. They put their ponies in the Harleys' paddock and walked across the Town Green to the Klines'. Mimi and Rosalie were sitting at the picnic table on the deck behind the house. Both girls were doing an art project.

Mimi held up a blue construction-paper star that was decorated with gold sparkles.

"I'm making prizes for a pretend horse show," Mimi told them.

The Pony Pals admired the prizes.

"And what about you, Rosalie?" asked Anna. "What are you making?"

Rosalie held up a long string with a ball of aluminum foil paper tied to one end.

"I'm making toys for Chicago," she explained. "He's my cat."

"Did your mother say you can have a cat?" asked Anna.

"She will," answered Rosalie. "When I ask her."

Lulu and Pam exchanged a worried look. Rosalie was still convinced she could adopt the black-and-white kitten. They needed to distract her.

"Can Rosalie have the first riding lesson today?" Pam asked Mimi.

"Sure," said Mimi. "She can win the first prize. I'll give it to her."

Anna helped Mimi make prizes while Lulu and Pam gave Rosalie her lesson. Pam brought a riding crop for Rosalie to use on Tongo.

Rosalie worked hard at controlling the difficult pony, but he still wanted to walk slowly and stop to eat grass whenever he pleased.

After the lesson, the Pony Pals went back to Anna's and saddled up their ponies. Then they rode on Pony Pal Trail to the Crandals'. Pony Pal Trail was a mile-and-a-half trail through the woods. It connected the paddock behind Anna's house to the Crandals' big field.

When they reached Pam's they went to the barn office to check for e-mail.

"It's here!" Pam shouted excitedly. "Eleanor has answered our message."

"Read it," said Anna.

Pam clicked the computer mouse twice and Eleanor's e-mail message appeared on the screen. Lulu read it out loud.

Dear Pony Pals: I loved receiving your e-mail. Starfire and I would be happy to participate in your benefit for St. Francis

Animal Shelter. Thank you for inviting us. Anna, I do remember meeting you. You had curly blonde hair and loved ponies. I am glad to hear that you now have your own pony and look forward to meeting Acorn. Lulu, I haven't met you, but Pam's mother told me all about you and Snow White. I'll be seeing you tomorrow. Receiving your e-mail made me happy.

Bye for now. Eleanor.

The Pony Pals shouted, "Yes!" and hit high fives.

"This is so great!" exclaimed Lulu.

"And it will be fun," added Anna.

"Uh-oh," said Pam.

"What's wrong?" Anna asked.

"How are we going to let people know Eleanor is performing?" she said. "The posters don't say anything about an Olympic jumper."

"Good point," said Lulu.

"Maybe we could add something to the

poster," suggested Anna. "Like a banner across the bottom."

"That's a good idea. We should do it right away," Pam said. "I'll go tell my mother that Eleanor's coming. You two work on the banner."

An hour later the Pony Pals were on their way back to town with bright orange banners.

☆ SHOW JUMPING EXHIBITION BY FAMOUS ☆
☆ OLYMPIC MEDAL WINNER ☆
☆ ELEANOR MORGAN AND STARFIRE! ☆

The girls rode to the diner first. Lulu taped the banner across the bottom of the poster while Anna and Pam got them a brownie snack.

Next, they went to the Green Market. Pam was pinning the banner to the community bulletin board when she heard a familiar voice. She looked over her shoulder and saw Mrs. Lacey, Rosalie and her brother Mike standing near the vegetable section. Tears streamed down Rosalie's face. Mrs. Lacey was speaking to her children in a low, angry voice.

Lulu motioned to Pam and Anna to move closer so they could hear what Mrs. Lacey was saying. They stood, half-hidden, behind the pasta section.

"Chicago is my kitty," Rosalie said between sobs. "I have to take care of him."

"How many times do I have to tell you," Mrs. Lacey scolded. "Cat food is expensive. Cats are a lot of trouble. And then there's the kitty litter. Which not only costs money, but stinks." She shook a finger at Mike. "And you. Why did you bring her to the shelter in the first place? You should know better."

Mike spotted the Pony Pals and pointed at them. "They brought her there first," he shouted. "It's their fault!"

Rosalie saw the Pony Pals, too. She ran over and threw her arms around Pam's waist.

SPECIAL
PASTA
PASTA

"Tell her," Rosalie begged. "Tell her that Chicago is my kitty."

Mrs. Lacey glared at the Pony Pals. "Don't encourage Rosalie in this cat thing," she said. "She can ride your ponies, but NO PETS!"

An elderly woman tapped Mrs. Lacey on the shoulder. "Could you weigh these apples for me?" she asked.

"Certainly," Mrs. Lacey said in a calmer voice. "Sorry to make you wait." She took the bag from the woman and went back to the fruit and vegetable section.

Mike Lacey glared at the Pony Pals. Mike was an eighth grader, who could be a real bully—especially when he hung out with his pal, Tommy Rand.

"You really are the Pony Pests," he said.

Anna put her hands on her hips and glared right back at him. "Stop calling us that," she warned.

"We're nice to your sister," said Lulu. "You should be, too."

"Don't tell me what to do," Mike snarled. "She's *my* sister."

Rosalie ran back to her brother's side and took his hand. "Mike saw Chicago," she said. "He thinks he's a cute kitten, don't you, Mike?"

"Yeah," said Mike. "He's pretty cute. But you heard what Ma said."

Pam was glad to see that Mike was at least being nice to Rosalie. She always thought Mike was much nicer when he wasn't around his big hero, Tommy Rand.

"Did you tell Mike about the horse show?" Lulu asked Rosalie.

Rosalie nodded. "But Tongo doesn't behave," she said.

"We'll work on that some more," Pam told her.

Poor Rosalie, thought Pam, it will be hard for her to win a ribbon on Tongo. Pam didn't believe in competitions and prizes for herself. But she suddenly wanted Rosalie Lacey to win that blue ribbon.

5

Starfire

The next day the Pony Pals gave Rosalie and Mimi another lesson with Tongo. Both girls worked hard. Tongo did not.

After the lesson, Pam rode home on Pony Pal Trail. She kept Lightning at a slow walk and enjoyed riding alone through the woods. She thought about how much she'd loved horses and riding. Competitions and prizes were all right for some people, but not for her.

As they came off the trail Pam leant forward. "Let's go," she told Lightning. They galloped across the field. Suddenly, Pam saw an amazing sight. A horse and rider were flying through the air above the big paddock. Pam slowed Lightning to a walk. The horse had landed on the other side of a high jump.

The rider spotted Pam and waved to her. It was Eleanor Morgan and Starfire!

Pam galloped Lightning over to the paddock. Eleanor and Starfire were waiting for them at the fence.

"Hello there," said Eleanor.

Pam hadn't seen Eleanor in person for a couple of years. She felt shy and excited at the same time.

"I saw you jump," Pam said. "It was so beautiful. You're great."

Eleanor smiled. "I was just going to say the same thing about your riding," she said. "You ride beautifully, too."

"I love to ride," said Pam.

"What about jumping?" asked Eleanor.

Pam nodded. "Jumping's the best."

Lightning reached over the fence and sniffed at Starfire's face. Starfire sniffed back.

"Lightning is friendly," said Eleanor.

"Starfire is, too," said Pam.

Pam loved that Starfire was the same chestnut color as Lightning and had a white marking on his forehead. Starfire's marking was a star.

"If I lowered the jump rails, would you jump Lightning for me?" asked Eleanor.

"Okay," agreed Pam.

Pam was nervous about jumping in front of an Olympic champion. But after the first jump that feeling went away. She thought only about Eleanor's riding and jumping tips. Pam loved having Eleanor for a teacher.

A half hour later Eleanor motioned Pam to ride over to her. Pam pulled up Lightning in front of their new teacher.

Eleanor rubbed Lightning's upside-down heart. "Well done, Lightning," she said. She smiled at Pam. "You, too. But we should stop for today."

Pam slid off Lightning and slipped the reins over the pony's head. "Thank you for

the lesson," Pam told Eleanor. "I can groom Starfire for you."

"Thanks, but I like to groom him myself," Eleanor said. "Starfire's my best friend."

"I feel the same way about Lightning," Pam said.

Pam and Eleanor led Lightning and Starfire into the barn.

"I can work with you tomorrow, too," Eleanor told Pam. "Maybe you'll win the championship trophy at the horse show."

"I'm not going to be in the horse show," Pam told her.

Eleanor looked surprised. "Don't you and your friends like to be in horse shows?"

"Anna and Lulu do," said Pam. "But I don't."

"I see," said Eleanor thoughtfully. She didn't say anything else until they were cooling down their animals. "You know, Pam, being in horse shows isn't only about winning prizes. It's about having a good time and observing other riders. We learn from one another that way."

"Do you like the prize part?" Pam asked.

"Sure I do," said Eleanor. "But I enjoy riding and jumping when there aren't prizes, too."

Pam and Eleanor were walking towards the house when Pam's mother returned from shopping. Mrs. Crandal stepped out of the car and walked towards them, waving.

"Your mother and I had the best time growing up together," Eleanor told Pam. "And we had such a good time when I arrived today. We're still best friends."

Best friends forever, thought Pam. That's the way I'll be with Anna and Lulu.

Mrs. Crandal met them. "Did you have a good workout with Starfire?" she asked Eleanor.

"Yes," Eleanor said. "I also saw what your talented daughter can do with her pony."

"She gave me a lesson," Pam added.

"Lucky for you," Pam's mother told her.

Eleanor told Mrs. Crandal all the good things she'd noticed about Pam's riding.

"Too bad she doesn't like to show it off,"

Mrs. Crandal said. "I don't understand that about Pam."

When they reached the house Pam went right to her room. She threw herself across the bed, rolled over and looked at the ceiling. What's wrong with me? she thought. Everyone else likes horse shows.

Pam could hear her mother and Eleanor talking in the kitchen. She thought she heard her name. Pam wondered what they were saying about her. So she crept down the stairs and stood near the kitchen door to listen.

"Pam's been in horse shows," her mother was saying, "and did very well. But it's always a struggle to get her to compete. Now she flatly refuses."

"Maybe she's afraid that she won't win," suggested Eleanor.

"I bet you're right," Mrs. Crandal said. "She's afraid to lose."

"It's a shame," said Eleanor, "because she's a very gifted rider. A natural talent."

"Do you think she could be a professional rider?" Mrs. Crandal asked.

"Absolutely," Eleanor said. "She's one of the best young riders I've worked with. It's really a shame that she doesn't like showing."

The two women were quiet for a few seconds.

"Let's go out to the barn," Pam's mother said. "I want to show you my new school ponies. They're really cute."

Pam quickly ran upstairs before her mother found her eavesdropping. She went to her room and quietly closed the door. Tears sprang to her eyes. They were a mixture of happy tears and sad tears. The happy ones were because Eleanor thought she could be a great rider. The sad ones were because she knew her mother was right. She was afraid of losing.

Junior Pony Pals

After breakfast the next morning, Pam went out to saddle up Lightning. She saw Lightning and Starfire nose to nose in the large paddock. Suddenly, Starfire broke into a canter and ran along the paddock fence line. Lightning whinnied happily and followed him. Pam sat on the fence and watched the beautiful animals. She thought, I want to be with ponies and horses forever. They are the most important thing in my life.

"Hi, there," a voice called.

Pam turned to see Eleanor Morgan

walking towards her. Eleanor leant on the fence beside Pam and they watched Starfire and Lightning together.

"Thanks again for the lesson yesterday," Pam told Eleanor. "I loved it."

"How would you like another one this afternoon?" asked Eleanor.

"That'd be great!" exclaimed Pam.

Pam called Lightning and brought her to the barn. As she saddled up her pony she thought about Rosalie Lacey. Today was Rosalie's last lesson before the horse show. Pam hoped she could be as good a riding teacher for Rosalie as Eleanor was for her.

An hour later the Pony Pals and Lightning were in the Klines' backyard giving riding lessons.

Tongo was in a stubborn, lazy mood. Anna scolded and pulled on the lead until Tongo finally walked around the yard.

Mimi followed the directions Lulu gave her. She sat tall and still in the saddle, kept her heels down and her toes up, and looked straight ahead. Maybe she will win a blue ribbon for lead line, thought Pam.

While Mimi rode Tongo, Rosalie practiced on Lightning. First, Pam had Rosalie practice Walk and Halt. Pam was amazed that the little girl remembered everything.

Next, Rosalie posted to the trot. She posted as if she'd been doing it all her life.

"Rosalie has a natural riding talent," Pam whispered to Lulu. "She's very gifted."

"I wish her mother and brother would see how good she is," said Lulu.

After Mimi's lesson, Rosalie rode Tongo. Her riding wasn't as good as it had been on Lightning. Tongo's trot was so slow that Rosalie couldn't post.

"It's not your fault," Pam told her. "Tongo is a very difficult pony."

"I won't win a ribbon," Rosalie said.

"You'll have lots of fun at the horse show, even if you don't win a ribbon," Pam told her.

"I know," said Rosalie. She leaned over

and hugged Tongo. "I still love you, Tongo. You'll be better tomorrow."

Pam knew that wasn't true. Tongo was an old, stubborn pony. He would never be a co-operative school pony like Lightning.

Pam checked her watch. Her lesson with Eleanor was in an hour.

"Your riding lessons are over," she told Rosalie and Mimi. "We'll see you at the horse show tomorrow."

As Rosalie was getting off Tongo, a neighbor's cat wriggled under the fence and ran around the yard.

"Look at the cat!" shouted Mimi.

Rosalie saw the cat and burst into tears.

"What's wrong, Rosalie?" Anna asked.

"Chicago can't go anywhere," she cried. "He lives in a cage."

Mimi came over and put an arm around her friend's shoulder. "Don't cry," she said.

"Chicago doesn't have a mother and father," Rosalie sobbed. "No one wants him."

"You want him," Mimi said. "You're not nobody."

"But I can't have him," Rosalie wailed.

The Pony Pals exchanged a glance. They had to do something for Rosalie.

"I have an idea," said Anna. "How would you girls like to be Junior Pony Pals."

"Pony Pals!" exclaimed Mimi with delight.

"Could we?" asked Rosalie in amazement.

"You can have Pony Pal meetings," said Lulu.

"Pony Pals do lots of neat stuff," said Mimi.

"Can we have a Junior Pony Pal meeting right now?" asked Mimi.

"Junior Pony Pals can have a meeting whenever they want," explained Anna.

"You can talk about the horse show at your meeting," said Lulu. "Then give Tongo a good grooming. You want him to be very beautiful for the horse show tomorrow."

"Pony Pals take care of animals," said Rosalie sadly. "But I can't take care of Chicago."

I have to think of a way to help Rosalie, thought Pam. There has to be a solution to Rosalie's problems.

The three older girls left the Klines' and led Lightning across the Town Green to Anna's.

"What are we going to do about Rosalie?" asked Lulu.

"It's time for three ideas," said Anna.

"I have to go home now," Pam said. "But come over to my place later. We can have a Pony Pal Meeting to share our ideas. And you can meet Eleanor and Starfire."

Lulu and Anna agreed to the plan. As they all walked across the Harleys' paddock toward the entrance to Pony Pal Trail, Pam told them about her lessons with Eleanor.

"Does that mean you'll be in the horse show?" asked Anna.

"My mother and Eleanor think I should," said Pam. "But I don't want to."

"You won't get chicken pox again," said Anna with a laugh.

"I know," said Pam. She mounted Lightning and Lulu opened the gate to Pony Pal Trail.

Pam waved goodbye to her friends and rode along the trail. She remembered how much she hated the first horse show she was ever in. When the show was over and she took off her shirt, she discovered that she was covered with itchy, red spots. She had chicken pox. Anna and Lulu decided that she hated that first horse show because she was sick. But Pam knew now she didn't like horse shows because she was afraid of losing. I want to stop being afraid, she thought. I want to enter horse shows to have fun. But can I, she wondered?

Three Ideas

Pam was having a terrific riding lesson. Every tip Eleanor gave her about jumping worked.

"Okay," Eleanor called. "Let's see you do all three jumps this time."

As Pam trotted Lightning towards the first jump, she saw that she had an audience. Her mother, her father, her six-year-old twin sister and brother—Jack and Jill—were lined up along the fence watching her. Anna and Lulu were there, too.

"Okay, Lightning," Pam told her pony. "Let's go."

When Pam and Lightning completed the jumps, everyone applauded.

"She's good!" Jack shouted.

"She jumped so-oo high!" exclaimed Jill.

Anna and Lulu shouted, "Yes!"

Pam knew that she and Lightning had done three perfect jumps in a row. She was glad that her family and best friends had seen it. It was fun to show what she and Lightning could do.

Eleanor raised the jump rails to the next level. Pam galloped Lightning up to the first jump. They flew over it. And the next. And the last.

The audience applauded and screamed with excitement.

This is so much fun, thought Pam.

Eleanor was beaming with happiness, too. "A nice ending to a great lesson," she told Pam as the young rider slid off her pony.

Anna and Lulu came over to meet Eleanor and talk about the horse show. Mrs.

Crandal invited everyone to come to the house for a snack.

Afterwards the Pony Pals walked back to the barn for their Pony Pal Meeting.

"Your jumping was great today," Lulu told Pam. "You could probably win the championship trophy at the horse show."

"But what if I don't win it?" said Pam. "Then my mother and Eleanor will be disappointed in me. Especially Eleanor."

"They'd still be proud of you," said Anna. "And you'd have fun."

Pam thought about what Anna had said. It had been fun to jump in front of an audience. And she liked the idea of everyone seeing her wonderful pony. Suddenly, Pam realized she wanted to be in the horse show. Maybe she'd even win the championship trophy. Eleanor would be so happy if she did.

"I'll be in the horse show," Pam told her friends. "I'll enter the equitation division. I really want to do it now."

"All-right!" shouted Pam and Lulu.

The three friends climbed the ladder to

the hayloft. They sat around the haybale table for their meeting about Rosalie.

"Here's the problem," Lulu began. "Rosalie Lacey wants to adopt an orphaned kitten, but her mother won't let her."

"Rosalie has other problems with her family," said Anna. "Her father lives in Chicago and she misses him."

"And she's going to be in a horse show tomorrow on a stubborn pony," added Pam. "Rosalie is a great little rider, but no one can tell when she's riding Tongo."

"Rosalie has three problems," concluded Lulu. "What are we going to do about them?"

"I have a solution for the problem with Tongo," said Pam. She took out a piece of paper and read:

Rosalie can ride Lightning at the horse show.

"But you're riding Lightning in the horse show," said Anna.

"We can both ride her," said Pam. "We won't be riding at the same time. Rosalie is only entering one class. I want her to be great in it."

"Especially if my idea works," said Anna.

"What is it?" asked Lulu.

Anna unfolded a piece of drawing paper and laid it out on the table.

"We have to get Mrs. Lacey and Mike to go to the horse show," Anna explained. "It would be so great for Rosalie if her family was there. We should talk to Mike about it."

"Good idea," said Pam.

"I'll take photos of her at the horse show," suggested Lulu. "She can send them to her father in Chicago."

"Chicago," said Lulu. "That reminds me of my idea." She handed Pam a small, open notebook. Pam read Lulu's idea out loud.

Ask Mrs. and Mr. Kline to adopt Chicago. Rosalie can help take care of him.

"That's a terrific idea," Pam said. "If Chicago lived right next door, Rosalie could see him all the time. It will be like it's *her* kitten."

"And he can be a stablemate for Tongo," said Anna.

"Well, my idea is easy to make happen," said Pam. "But we have to work on the other two ideas."

"Let's go to town and try to find Mike," suggested Lulu.

"He's probably shooting baskets in the schoolyard," said Anna. "That's what he and Tommy have been doing all summer."

"Should we talk to Mrs. Lacey?" wondered Lulu.

"I don't think so," said Anna. "She already thinks we're troublemakers. It's better if Mike asks her."

"First, let's call the Klines at the hardware store," suggested Pam, "and talk to Mr. and Mrs. Kline about adopting Chicago."

"You make the call, Pam," suggested Anna.

The Pony Pals went down the ladder and into Mrs. Crandal's office. Pam called the hardware store, but the Klines weren't there. Next, Pam called their house. Mrs. Bell, Mimi's babysitter, answered the phone.

"Mr. and Mrs. Kline aren't here," Mrs. Bell told Pam. "They are on a buying trip for the store. They won't be back until tomorrow morning—just in time for the horse show."

Pam said thank you and goodbye to Mrs.

Bell. She hung up the phone and told Anna and Lulu the bad news.

"Then we can't ask them about adopting Chicago until tomorrow," said Lulu.

Pam hoped they would have better luck finding Mike Lacey. They had to convince Mrs. Lacey and Mike to come to the horse show to see Rosalie ride Lightning.

The Big Choice

The Pony Pals rode to town, down Main Street and over to the schoolyard. Four guys were shooting baskets.

"Mike is here," said Pam.

"And Tommy is not," observed Lulu.

"Good," said Anna and motioned for Mike to come over.

The girls got off their ponies.

"What do you want?" Mike yelled.

"To tell you something," Lulu shouted back.

Mike ignored the Pony Pals while he tried for two more baskets.

"He just wants to look like a big shot who ignores girls," Anna told Pam and Lulu. "He'll come over. Eventually."

The three girls stood by their ponies and waited.

After Mike made another basket he finally walked over to them. "What do you want to tell me?" he asked.

"Rosalie is going to be in the horse show tomorrow," Pam told him.

"So what?" Mike asked.

"So, are you and your mother coming?" asked Anna.

"Don't know," replied Mike.

"It would make Rosalie so happy if you did," said Pam.

"She's been very sad lately," said Lulu. "She misses your father."

"And she wants to have that kitten," added Anna.

Mike nodded. "I know," he said. "She's been crying a lot."

He almost sounds like a human being, thought Pam. Now, if we can just convince him to go to the horse show and bring his mother.

"Hey, Pony Pests," someone shouted.

Pam looked across the schoolyard. Tommy Rand was coming towards them.

"The Pony Pests are here!" Mike shouted to Tommy. "Call an exterminator."

Mike whipped around and ran towards Tommy. Someone threw Mike the basketball. Mike threw it to Tommy. And they were both in the game.

"That's it," said Lulu. "He won't listen to us anymore. Tommy-the-Big-Dude is here."

The Pony Pals left the schoolyard and walked back to Anna's.

"Mike and his mother *might* come to the horse show," said Lulu. "We just won't know until tomorrow."

"At least we know Rosalie will do well in the show," said Anna. "Thanks to Pam."

"And Lightning," added Pam.

I'll ride Lightning in the show, too, thought Pam. She couldn't wait for tomorrow to come. She knew Eleanor and her friends were right. She had a good chance of winning that championship trophy.

The next morning Eleanor and Pam gave Starfire and Lightning an extra special grooming. Then they rode together to the Olsons' farm.

As they came up to the horse show, Pam's heart pounded with excitement. The field was already filled with trailers, horses and riders. Two rings were set up for the events, the volunteer firemen had a food stand, and a big banner over the entrance read, "Welcome Eleanor Morgan and Starfire!" The horse show was going to be a big success.

Mr. Olson saw Eleanor and Pam and ran over to greet them.

"Come to the judges' table, Eleanor," he said. "There are some people who want to meet you and Starfire."

"Good luck," Pam told Eleanor. "I can't wait to see you jump again."

"Good luck to you, too," Eleanor told Pam. "I can't wait to see you jump again, either."

Pam smiled. Being in the horse show was already fun.

Pam dismounted and went to look for Lulu and Anna. As she led Lightning through the field she spotted a small tent with a sign that read, "Animals for Adoption."

Anna came out of the tent. Pam waved. Anna came over to her.

"The animal shelter had such a good idea," Anna told Pam. "They brought animals here that need homes. Maybe some will be adopted today."

"Uh-oh," said Pam. "Is Chicago here?"

Anna nodded. "Lots of people are looking at the kittens."

"I hope no one adopts Chicago before we talk to Mrs. Kline," said Pam. She looked around. "Is she here yet?"

"Not yet," said Anna. "Lulu and I brought Tongo, Mimi and Rosalie. Mrs. Bell helped."

"Did you tell Rosalie that she's riding Lightning?" asked Pam.

Anna nodded. "That's why she's so excited."

"Does she know Chicago is here?" asked Pam.

"Not yet," said Anna.

"Good," said Pam. "Let's try to keep it that way."

Anna took care of Lightning, while Pam signed up for the two equitation events. Then they joined Lulu and the Junior Pony Pals.

Pam let Rosalie help her with Lightning, while Anna and Mimi took care of Tongo and Acorn. Lulu led Snow White around the grounds and looked for Mr. and Mrs. Kline and Mike and Mrs. Lacey.

When Lulu returned, she came over to Pam. "I didn't see them," she whispered. "No Laceys. No Klines."

"Walk, Trot and Canter. Equitation Class. In ring number one," Mr. Olson announced over the loudspeaker.

Mrs. Bell took care of Tongo so Rosalie and Mimi could watch the Pony Pals in their first event. As Pam rode Lightning into the ring she thought, I want to win. Then she put that idea out of her mind and concentrated on riding well. When she finished, she knew she and Lightning had done their best. If the best wasn't good enough for a blue ribbon, that would be okay.

The girls and their ponies lined up across the center of the ring for their prizes.

Mr. Olson announced the winners and Eleanor gave out the ribbons.

Anna came in fourth. Lulu won third place. A girl from the next town won second.

"And the first place ribbon goes to Pam Crandal and her pony, Lightning," Mr. Olson announced. Eleanor winked at Pam when she gave her the blue ribbon.

They all left the ring. People were congratulating Pam when the loudspeaker went on again.

"We've had a fabulous turnout today, folks," Mr. Olson announced. "So we're using two rings for the next events."

"That's great," said Anna. "They must be making a lot of money for the shelter!"

"In ring one we'll have Equitation Jumping.

In ring two we'll have Walk, Trot. Contestants, line up, please."

Rosalie pulled on Pam's hand. "Walk, Trot," she said. "That's me and Lightning. I have to get my helmet."

I'm supposed to do Equitation Jumping on Lightning, thought Pam. She and Rosalie both needed Lightning at the same time. What was she going to do?

Blue Ribbons

Rosalie ran over to Mimi and Mrs. Bell to tell them she was next. Anna and Lulu came over to Pam.

"Pam, what are you going to do?" asked Lulu. "Lightning can't be in two competitions at once."

"If you don't jump, you can't win the trophy," said Anna.

"I know," replied Pam. She felt a little sick in her stomach. She had already told Rosalie she could ride Lightning in the horse show. And Rosalie had her heart set on winning a ribbon.

"Rosalie can ride Acorn," suggested Anna. "I don't have a chance of winning the trophy, anyway."

Pam shook her head. "Rosalie hasn't ridden Acorn in a long time. She'll do her best riding on Lightning."

Rosalie and Mimi ran up to the Pony Pals.

"My mother is here!" Rosalie shrieked. "She came to see me ride."

"Mike came, too!" added Mimi.

Pam made her decision. "Rosalie is riding Lightning," she told Anna and Lulu.

Anna and Lulu were sorry that Pam wasn't going to compete for the trophy. But Pam knew that they would have made the same decision.

"Good luck, Rosalie," said Anna.

"Focus on your riding, not on the audience," Lulu advised.

Anna and Lulu rode up to ring number one to enter Equitation Jumping. Pam helped Rosalie mount Lightning. As she walked them over to ring number two, Pam reviewed some riding tips with the young rider.

"I'm scared," Rosalie told Pam. "How come I'm scared?"

"It's normal," Pam told her. "Just focus on your riding. Don't think about anything else."

Pam gave Lightning a little pat. Rosalie rode into the ring and the class began.

Mimi and Mrs. Bell stood with Pam by the fence.

"Is she going to win?" Mimi asked Pam.

"I don't know," Pam said. "The important thing is that she rides well and has a good time."

Rosalie and Lightning rode by them. They circled the ring at a walk. Pam thought they made a perfect team.

"You're doing great," Pam told her. "Keep it up."

"Go, Rosalie, go!" cheered Mimi.

Next, the riders posted to the trot. Rosalie passed them again.

"She rides so good," Mimi said.

"What a lovely sight it is," said Mrs. Bell.

Pam hoped that the judges would think so, too.

At the end of the event the riders lined up across the ring. It was time to announce prizes. Eleanor went into the ring to distribute them. She must be disappointed that I'm not jumping, thought Pam.

Mr. Olson announced fourth place, then third, then second. Rosalie won none of them. Finally Mr. Olson said, "The first place prize, the blue ribbon . . . goes to Rosalie Lacey on Pam Crandal's pony, Lightning."

The audience applauded. Mimi jumped up and down screaming excitedly. In all that noise Pam heard Mike Lacey shout, "All right, Rosalie!"

Rosalie leaned over to take the ribbon from Eleanor. She smiled and held it up for everyone to see.

Eleanor left the ring and walked over to Pam. "I wondered why you weren't jumping," she said. "Now I know."

"I promised Rosalie she could ride

Lightning today," said Pam. "I didn't know her event would be at the same time as jumping."

"You did the right thing," Eleanor said. "For that little girl, this is very special."

"I'll be in a lot of other horse shows," Pam said.

"I'm glad to hear it," said Eleanor. "I have to go and give out the prizes in jumping, but as far as I'm concerned you are the big winner today."

After Eleanor left, Pam went to meet Rosalie on Lightning.

Mrs. Lacey, Mike, all the Klines, Mrs. Bell, Pam's mother and Jack and Jill were all gathered around them.

The first thing Pam noticed was that Mrs. Lacey was actually smiling. "You looked so fine out there," she told Rosalie. "Aren't you afraid of that big animal?"

Rosalie shook her head no. "I love her!" she exclaimed. She dismounted and put the ribbon on Lightning's bridle. "It's Lightning's ribbon."

"But you'll keep it for her," Pam told Rosalie.

"Okay," Rosalie agreed.

Mr. Olson was back on the loudspeaker announcing the winners in equitation jumping. Anna won the second place ribbon in jumping and Lulu the third. The girl who won second prize in Walk, Trot and Canter won first prize in jumping. So she'll win the big trophy, thought Pam. "In ring number one," Mr. Olson continued, "Lead Line."

"It's your turn," Rosalie told Mimi. "Let's go."

The whole group walked over to ring one. Rosalie led Lightning. Pam and Mimi led Tongo. Anna and Lulu were waiting for them. They hugged and congratulated Rosalie. And everyone congratulated the older girls also.

"I'm going to win a ribbon, too," Mimi announced. "A blue one. Tongo and me."

Tongo took one look at the crowd around the ring and shook his head as if to say, "No way. I'm not going out there."

"Tongo is in a super stubborn mood," Anna whispered to Pam.

"Tell him who's boss," Pam told her.

Anna took Tongo's bridle and pulled up his head. She looked into the small pony's eyes. "You are going out there and doing what I say," she said in a stern voice. Tongo tried to drop his head so he wouldn't have to look at Anna. She wouldn't let him. "You will behave," she said. "Don't let Mimi down."

"Lead Line entrants, walk around the ring," announced Mr. Olson. "Leave three pony-lengths between ponies. Keep that distance throughout the competition."

Pam helped Mimi mount Tongo.

"Let Tongo know you're in charge," Pam told her.

Anna led Tongo and Mimi into the ring. Tongo tried to stop. Pam saw Mimi give Tongo a firm heel in the side.

Tongo walked on.

"Look at her," Pam heard Mrs. Kline tell her husband. "She's learning how to control him."

Mrs. Kline was right. Mimi stayed focused and Tongo behaved. Once Mimi looked over at her family and friends and waved. But otherwise she kept all her attention on riding.

The twelve contestants walked around the ring three times then lined up across the center. It was time for prizes.

"This was an outstanding demonstration of Lead Line," Mr. Olson announced. "Everyone in this competition will win a blue ribbon."

"Yea!" shouted someone in the crowd.

"They do that a lot for Lead Line," Mrs. Crandal told the Pony Pals.

The audience cheered and clapped. Eleanor handed out a blue ribbon to each of the riders. Mimi held her ribbon high for everyone to see.

"In ten minutes we'll have the jumping demonstration by Olympic champion, Eleanor Morgan," Mr. Olson announced. "Also, there are animals for adoption in the tent behind the food stand. Three dogs and two cats are left. All the black-and-white kittens have been adopted. They will be there until the end of the show. Those kittens are very cute, so go on over and see them. And check out the other pets while you are there."

"My kitty!" Rosalie exclaimed. "Someone took Chicago!" She broke away from the group of family and friends and ran into the crowd.

Show Time!

Pam ran after Rosalie. She caught up with her at the animal shelter tent. Rosalie was already there, bent over the cage of kittens.

"Chicago," she sobbed. "I wanted to take care of you."

Pam knelt down beside Rosalie. "He'll have a good home, Rosalie," she said. "He won't be in a cage anymore. Aren't you happy for him?"

"Maybe some other time you can have a cat," said a boy behind Pam. Pam looked up. It was Mike. He knelt down beside his sister.

"I asked Ma to let you have him," he said. "I told her I'd get a job to pay for the food and everything."

Rosalie looked up at her brother. "You did?"

"Course I did," said Mike.

"But she wouldn't let me have him," said Rosalie sadly.

"She doesn't like cats," said Mike.

Mrs. Kline came into the tent. She joined the little group around the cage. "You have to understand, Rosalie," Mrs. Kline said. "Some people don't like animals as much as other people."

"When I'm a grown up I'm going to have millions of animals," said Rosalie. She poked a finger into the cage. Chicago came over and sniffed it.

"Maybe you should find out who adopted him," Mrs. Kline said. "Maybe it's someone who lives very close to you. Then you could visit him whenever you want."

Rosalie looked up at Mrs. Kline. "Do you know who adopted him?" she asked.

Mrs. Kline nodded.

"Who?" Rosalie asked.

Mrs. Kline smiled at Rosalie and leaned over to whisper something in her ear.

Rosalie threw her arms around Mrs. Kline's neck and hugged her.

Mrs. Kline looked up at Pam and Mike. "We adopted Chicago," she told them. "For Mimi and Rosalie. But, of course, he'll live at our place."

"If he's at your house," Rosalie said, "I can help take care of him."

"That's right," agreed Mrs. Kline. "We'll pick him up after the horse show and take him home."

Rosalie stared in amazement at the black-and-white kitty. "Mimi and me have a kitty," she said happily. She sat on the ground in front of the cage. "I'm going to stay here until the horse show is over."

"Don't you want to tell Mimi about the

kitten," said Mrs. Kline. "She doesn't know yet."

"I'll tell her," squealed Rosalie. "I'll tell her."

A voice came over the loudspeaker. "Eleanor Morgan and Starfire are ready to perform in the first ring."

"Let's go," Pam said. "Or we'll miss it."

Rosalie jumped up. "I'll be back, Chicago," she said. "Mimi and me will come get you."

Pam found Anna and Lulu standing near the riding ring. Pam told Lulu and Anna the news about the kitten.

"Isn't that amazing?" Pam said. "Mrs. Kline had the same idea we had."

Anna and Lulu giggled.

"What's so funny?" asked Pam.

"We told her the idea," Lulu said. "When you were with Rosalie at the second ring. We didn't have time to tell you."

"And we didn't know if she would do it," added Anna.

"So all of our ideas worked!" exclaimed Pam.

Eleanor and Starfire entered the ring. Eleanor had on her U.S. team riding jacket. She cantered around and flew over three jumps in a row. Then she cantered around the ring and did it again.

I want to jump like that some day, thought Pam. I *can* jump like that some day. I *will*!

The crowd clapped long and hard. Lulu took out her camera. Eleanor did two more jumps. Lulu snapped some pictures. Pam couldn't wait to see them.

After the demonstration, Lulu took a photo of Rosalie with Lightning and their prize.

"I'm going to send that picture to my daddy," Rosalie said proudly. "He lives in Chicago."

Next, Lulu took a photo of Mimi and Tongo.

"Will you take a picture of Mimi and me and Chicago, too?" asked Rosalie.

"Sure," said Lulu. "As soon as you get him."

"Mimi's my best friend," Rosalie said. She put an arm around Mimi's shoulder. "We're Junior Pony Pals." Lulu snapped a picture.

The Pony Pals took photos of one another with their ponies and their prizes.

Pam hooked the ribbon she'd won with Lightning on his bridle. She put her arm around Lightning's neck. "You were great today," Pam told her pony. "I'm so proud of you."

She smiled at the camera. Lightning nickered a happy sound. And Lulu clicked the picture.

Dear Reader:

I am having a lot of fun researching and writing books about the Pony Pals. I've met many interesting kids and adults who love ponies. And I've visited some wonderful ponies at homes, farms, and riding schools.

Before writing Pony Pals I wrote fourteen novels for children and young adults. Four of these were honored by Children's Choice Awards.

I live in Sharon, Connecticut, with my husband, Lee, and our dog, Willie. Our daughter is all grown up and has her own apartment in New York City.

Besides writing novels I like to draw, paint, garden, and swim. I didn't have a pony when I was growing up, but I have always loved them and dreamt about riding. Now I take riding lessons on a horse named Saz.

I like reading and writing about ponies as much as I do riding. Which proves to me that you don't have to ride a pony to love them. And you certainly don't need a pony to be a Pony Pal.

Happy Reading,

Jeanne Betancourt